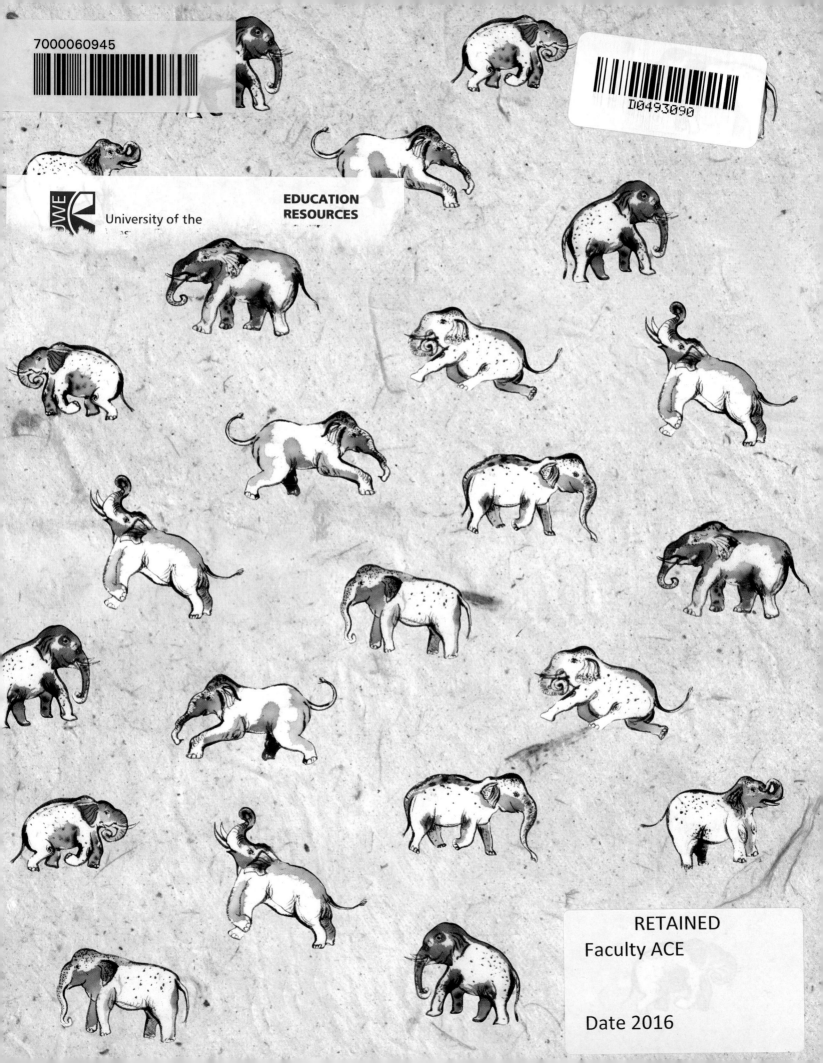

For Sai and Anna, the original Yi-Min — C.B.
For Florence — T.V.

ABOUT THE STORY

The story is set during the T'ang Dynasty (618-907 A.D.), a time of great prosperity in China. "White" elephants are extremely rare (most reference books describe them as "albino" or "pinkish-white") and have always been regarded as sacred in parts of Asia. The elephants living in ancient China were the Asiatic or Indian elephant, *Elephas Maximus*. They are slighter than African elephants, with smaller ears and tusks. Indian elephants used to be found in most of southern China, and as far north as the North Honan Province. Now an endangered species, threatened by human populations, they can still be found in the equatorial forest of Xishuangbanna.

Yi-Min and the Elephants copyright © Frances Lincoln Limited 2002
Text copyright © Caroline Heaton 2002
Illustrations copyright © Tim Vyner 2002

First published in Great Britain in 2002 by
Frances Lincoln Limited, 4 Torriano Mews
Torriano Avenue, London NW5 2RZ

www.franceslincoln.com

British Library Cataloguing in Publication Data
available on request

ISBN 0-7112-1852-8

Set in Fournier MT

Printed in Singapore

1 3 5 7 9 8 6 4 2

YI-MIN and the ELEPHANTS

A Tale of Ancient China

Caroline Heaton

Illustrated by Tim Vyner

FRANCES LINCOLN

T HERE ONCE LIVED in ancient China an Emperor who had three daughters.

The older two had long married and gone to live in neighbouring lands, but the youngest was still a child and remained at home.

Her name was Yi-Min and she was not only the youngest, but the smallest of the daughters. She was so small that she reached no higher than the toe-nail of the carved jade dragon which guarded the gates of her father's palace. And when I tell you that the dragon was barely four feet tall, you will see just how tiny she was.

Yi-Min's mother was dead and, as the youngest child, she was much indulged. While the ladies of the court tottered about on tiny bound feet, Yi-Min's feet were left unbound and she ran freely through the many rooms of the palace in slippers made from scraps of scarlet silk.

Above all, she loved to visit the Emperor's treasure-room, which contained among other things the silver horn of a unicorn and a living sea-horse in its own miniature ocean.

The Emperor collected rare objects as you might collect stamps. So when travellers told him of some white elephants in a far-flung corner of the empire, he immediately wanted one of their ivory tusks.

As soon as Yi-Min heard about the elephants she became very excited, for she had never seen such a creature before.

"What does an elephant look like, Papa?" she asked.

"Big," replied the Emperor. "As big as a house and as tall as a tree …"

Yi-Min's eyes widened.

"… with great long teeth," continued her father, "a huge nose and enormous ears."

"And are they fierce, Papa?"

Now the Emperor knew very little of the ways of elephants. However, he loved telling stories.

"… When they stampede," he said, "the dust rises for miles around. The pounding of their huge feet is like the drumming of a thousand drums. And when they bellow, it is like A THOUSAND TRUMPETS ECHOING …"

Yi-Min was curious to see such fabulous beasts, so she begged
her father to take her on an elephant hunt. The Emperor agreed
at once, and gave her a *shih-tzu*, the smallest palace dog, to ride on.

Then he hurried off to consult the palace astrologer, who
pulled out his old charts and pronounced it a good time for
journeys "... although," he added, "you may not find quite
what you seek."

The very next day the court set out, carrying flagons of rice
wine and many-flavoured teas.

Yi-Min was beginning to feel sleepy, for they had left very early, when a great silver-grey beast appeared ahead of them.

She took one look at its huge fangs and whispered, "The White Elephant!"

The courtiers roared with laughter. "No, no, that's a wolf!" they chorused. "An elephant is much bigger."

Yi-Min trembled with shame, and the Emperor reached down to tuck her into his sleeve. They rode on, with her little dog trotting behind.

They had not gone far when a great stripy beast crossed their path, baring his teeth in a fearsome snarl. Yi-Min could not imagine a bigger creature, and she called out, "The White Elephant!"

Once more, everyone laughed. "No, no, that's a tiger!"
they chorused. "An elephant is much bigger."
Yi-Min was astonished.

The company passed on into the mountains, and for a long time saw only wild goats and sheep. Then suddenly a great shaggy brown beast reared up in front of them.

It seemed to Yi-Min that he almost blocked the sky, but before she could speak, the courtiers told her it was a bear and they continued on their way.

By now, poor Yi-Min was beginning to wish she had stayed at home – when at last the courtiers set up a great cry.

There, in the distance, was a group of animals with soft grey
coats, gathered around a large pool. Certainly they were enormous,
but their huge, flapping ears and long, swaying trunks only made
Yi-Min laugh. They moved in a gentle, lumbering way and when
one of them sprayed water from its trunk, she clapped in delight.

Yi-Min was just about to run over to them, when she saw the courtiers raise their bows and arrows. The Emperor was giving the signal to fire.

"No!" cried Yi-Min. "Don't hurt them!"

Yi-Min's father looked at her in surprise. He ordered the
courtiers to lay down their bows.

"Daughter, these are the elephants we came to find …"

"But Papa, they're so beautiful," said Yi-Min, and a single tear,
the shape of her almond eyes, rolled down her cheek.

When the Emperor saw this, he was ashamed. "Perhaps you
would like to take one home instead?" he suggested, pointing to
a small elephant next to its mother.

"No," said Yi-Min firmly. "It's much happier here! But I would like to come back and see them again."

The Emperor thought for a moment. Then he said with a smile, "And so you shall. We will come every year on your birthday. And I will pass a new law forbidding the hunting of Yi-Min's Elephants!"

Yi-Min smiled back and everyone clapped. Then the company set off slowly for home, with Yi-Min and the shih-tzu perched up in front of the Emperor.

The rocking of the horse soon sent Yi-Min to sleep. And as she slept, she dreamt of creatures as big as houses and as tall as trees, padding softly with great feet over the earth.